Mr Mean lived up to his name.

He lived in what could have been a nice house, but wasn't.

He never painted it, or mended the windows, or repaired the roof.

Inside it was the same.

No carpets! No curtains! No pictures! No fires!

And Mr Mean was so mean he made his furniture out of old orange boxes, and then complained about the price of nails!

Why, he was so mean, do you know what he gave his brother for Christmas last year?

A piece of coal!

It wasn't as if Mr Mean didn't have any money.

Oh no!

He had lots of money, and he kept it all hidden in a box which he kept in the kitchen.

Every evening, he'd sit there counting it. It was the only thing Mr Mean liked doing.

But would he spend it?

Oh dear me, no.

Not old Meany.

Not if he could help it!

One day, Mr Mean was sitting in his gloomy kitchen having a gloomy meal.

He only ever had one meal a day, and that day, he was having a cup of water and a piece of bread which was three weeks old.

Suddenly, he was interrupted by a knock at the door.

"Drat!" he said, because he didn't like people. "Drat and bother!"

He opened the door, and there, on his doorstep, stood a wizard.

A rather fat wizard.

"Hello," said the wizard. "I wonder if, by any chance, as it's such a warm day, you could possibly, if it's not too much trouble, be so kind as to, if it's not inconvenient, perhaps, as I'm very thirsty, provide me with, do you think, a glass, if it's not too much to ask, of water, please?"

He was a very wordy wizard.

"No!" replied Mr Mean rudely, and shut the door in his face.

And went back into his kitchen to finish his meagre meal.

But there, standing in front of him, was the wizard.

"How did you get in?" gasped Mr Mean.

"Well," replied the wizard, "it was by, how shall I put it, I just, well, you know, waved the old whatsitsname, magic wand don't you know, and, well, here I am, if you know what I mean!"

"You must be very poor," he remarked kindly, looking around.

"Oh, yes I am," lied Mr Mean.

"Then perhaps I can help you," said the wizard, pulling up a box to sit down on.

The box didn't move, so the wizard pulled it harder, and this time it did move. In fact it tipped up and spilled all Mr Mean's money all over the floor.

"Well well well," exclaimed the wizard, eyeing the money rolling all over the kitchen floor. "Well well well well well well!"

"It would appear to me," he continued, "that you, sir, are an old Meany!"

Mr Mean didn't hear him.

He was too busy scrabbling all over the floor trying to pick up his money.

"And meanies," added the wizard, "need to be taught a lesson!"

So saying, he waved his magic wand.

All the money turned into potatoes!

Potatoes!

Poor Mr Mean.

"Oh! Oh dear! Oh dear me!" he wailed. "Please turn my money back into money. Oh please, please, please," he begged.

"Perhaps," replied the wizard. "But, on the other hand, taking all things into account, by and large, things being what they are, on the face of it, perhaps not."

"However," continued the wordy wizard, "if you make me a solemn promise never to be mean again, then I will turn your money back into money. But," he added sternly, "if you are ever mean again, then it's, how can I put it, then it's potatoes for you my lad. If not other vegetables as well!"

Then the wizard had the glass of water he'd come for in the first place, except it was a cup of water because Mr Mean didn't have any glasses.

Then, with another wave of his wand, he turned the potatoes back into money, and another wave of his wand made himself disappear.

"Stupid wizard," muttered Mr Mean, picking up all his money.

The following day, Mr Mean decided to walk to town.

He never took the bus because that cost money!

On the way, he met an old washerwoman carrying an enormous bundle of washing.

"Please kind sir," she asked, "could you possibly help me to carry this washing? It's so heavy!"

"No!" replied Mr Mean. "It's your washing. You carry it!"

But, as soon as he'd said that, he felt a tingling in his nose.

Mr Mean's nose turned into a carrot!

"Oh no!" he gasped.

The old washerwoman chuckled.

And then Mr Mean remembered the wizard's words.

"Yes! Yes!" he cried in a panic. "Of course I'll help you!"

And he carried the huge bundle of washing to where the old washerwoman wanted.

And the carrot turned back into a nose, and off he went.

The old washerwoman chuckled again, and turned back into the wizard.

It had been him all along!

On his way into town, Mr Mean passed by a cottage garden.

In the garden there was an old man chopping wood. He saw Mr Mean going past and called out.

"Excuse me," he called. "Could you give an old man a bit of a hand young fellow-me-lad?"

"No!" replied Mr Mean. "It's your wood. You chop it!"

But, as soon as the words had passed his lips, guess what happened?

His ears turned into tomatoes!!

"Oh no!" he gasped.

The old man chuckled.

And Mr Mean remembered the wizard's words.

"Yes! Yes!" he cried. "Of course I'll give you a hand."

And he chopped and chopped until all the wood was cut.

And the tomatoes turned back into ears, and off he went.

The old man chuckled again, and turned back into the wizard.

He was teaching Mr Mean a lesson, just as he'd promised.

Eventually Mr Mean arrived in the town.

There was a little boy crying because his ball had got stuck on top of a wall.

"Please sir," cried the boy. "Please sir, could you reach my ball down for me?"

"No!" retorted Mr Mean. "It's your ball. You . . ." Then he stopped.

There was a funny tingling feeling in his feet.

"Yes! Yes!" he said hurriedly. "Of course I will."

And he reached up and passed the ball to the boy, and went on his way, looking anxiously at his feet.

The little boy stopped crying and turned into the wizard.

"I think," he said to himself, "I think that Mr Mean, by and large, is beginning, if I'm not very much mistaken, to not be quite so mean, and, I think, although I could be wrong, although I never am, that he has, thank goodness, learned his lesson."

Today he's nothing like so mean as he used to be.

And he doesn't keep his money in a box in the kitchen any more.

He spent it all on having his house mended and painted and made spick and span.

And he's turned into quite a generous sort of a fellow.

Goodness, he's so generous, do you know what he gave his brother last Christmas?

Two pieces of coal!

3 Great Offers for MR.MEN Fans!

MR. MEN TOKEN

1 New Mr. Men or Little Miss Library Bus Presentation Cases

A brand new stronger, roomier school bus library box, with sturdy carrying handle and stay-closed fasteners.

The full colour, wipe-clean boxes make a great home for your full collection.

They're just £5.99 inc P&P and free bookmark!

☐ MR. MEN   ☐ LITTLE MISS (please tick and order overleaf)

2 Door Hangers and Posters

In every Mr. Men and Little Miss book like this one, you will find a special token. Collect 6 tokens and we will send you a brilliant Mr. Men or Little Miss poster and a Mr. Men or Little Miss double sided full colour bedroom door hanger of your choice. Simply tick your choice in the list and tape a 50p coin for your two items to this page.

PLEASE STICK YOUR 50P COIN HERE

Door Hangers (please tick)
☐ Mr. Nosey & Mr. Muddle
☐ Mr. Slow & Mr. Busy
☐ Mr. Messy & Mr. Quiet
☐ Mr. Perfect & Mr. Forgetful
☐ Little Miss Fun & Little Miss Late
☐ Little Miss Helpful & Little Miss Tidy
☐ Little Miss Busy & Little Miss Brainy
☐ Little Miss Star & Little Miss Fun

Posters (please tick)
☐ MR. MEN
☐ LITTLE MISS

3 Sixteen Beautiful Fridge Magnets – any 2 for £2.00! inc.P&P

They're very special collector's items!
Simply tick your first and second* choices from the list below
of any 2 characters!

1st Choice

- ☐ Mr. Happy
- ☐ Mr. Lazy
- ☐ Mr. Topsy-Turvy
- ☐ Mr. Bounce
- ☐ Mr. Bump
- ☐ Mr. Small
- ☐ Mr. Snow
- ☐ Mr. Wrong

- ☐ Mr. Daydream
- ☐ Mr. Tickle
- ☐ Mr. Greedy
- ☐ Mr. Funny
- ☐ Little Miss Giggles
- ☐ Little Miss Splendid
- ☐ Little Miss Naughty
- ☐ Little Miss Sunshine

2nd Choice

- ☐ Mr. Happy
- ☐ Mr. Lazy
- ☐ Mr. Topsy-Turvy
- ☐ Mr. Bounce
- ☐ Mr. Bump
- ☐ Mr. Small
- ☐ Mr. Snow
- ☐ Mr. Wrong

- ☐ Mr. Daydream
- ☐ Mr. Tickle
- ☐ Mr. Greedy
- ☐ Mr. Funny
- ☐ Little Miss Giggles
- ☐ Little Miss Splendid
- ☐ Little Miss Naughty
- ☐ Little Miss Sunshine

*Only in case your first choice is out of stock.

TO BE COMPLETED BY AN ADULT

**To apply for any of these great offers, ask an adult to complete the coupon below and send it with
the appropriate payment and tokens, if needed, to MR. MEN CLASSIC OFFER, PO BOX 715, HORSHAM RH12 5WG**

☐ Please send _____ Mr. Men Library case(s) and/or _____ Little Miss Library case(s) at £5.99 each inc P&P

☐ Please send a poster and door hanger as selected overleaf. I enclose six tokens plus a 50p coin for P&P

☐ Please send me _____ pair(s) of Mr. Men/Little Miss fridge magnets, as selected above at £2.00 inc P&P

Fan's Name _____

Address _____

_____ **Postcode** _____

Date of Birth _____

Name of Parent/Guardian _____

Total amount enclosed £ _____

☐ **I enclose a cheque/postal order payable to Egmont Books Limited**

☐ **Please charge my MasterCard/Visa/Amex/Switch or Delta account** (delete as appropriate)

Card Number

Expiry date ___/___ **Signature** _____

Please allow 28 days for delivery. Offer is only available while stocks last. We reserve the right to change the terms
of this offer at any time and we offer a 14 day money back guarantee. This does not affect your statutory rights.
Data Protection Act: If you do not wish to receive other similar offers from us or companies we recommend, please
tick this box ☐. Offers apply to UK only.

MR. MEN   LITTLE MISS
Mr. Men and Little Miss™ & ©Mrs. Roger Hargreaves

CUT ALONG DOTTED LINE AND RETURN THIS WHOLE PAGE